Freckles

Saddle Up Series
Book 26

Dave and Pat Sargent are longtime residents of Prairie Grove, Arkansas. Dave, a fourth-generation dairy farmer, began writing in early December of 1990. Pat, a former teacher, began writing in the fourth grade. They enjoy the outdoors and have a real love for animals.

Freckles

Saddle Up Series
Book 26

By Dave and Pat Sargent

Beyond "The End"
By Sue Rogers

Illustrated by Jane Lenoir

Ozark Publishing, Inc.
P.O. Box 228
Prairie Grove, AR 72753

Cataloging-in-Publication Data

Sargent, Dave, 1941—
    Freckles / by Dave and Pat Sargent ;
illustrated by Jane Lenoir.—Prairie Grove, AR :
Ozark Publishing, c2004.
        p. cm. (Saddle up series ; 26)

    "Be proud of Old Glory"—Cover.
    SUMMARY: On Independence Day at the
Rocking S Horse Ranch, a proud flea-bitten grey
horse, hoping to be chosen for a very special job,
tells a silver grullo how important horses have
been in United States history. Includes factual
information about flea-bitten grey horses.
        ISBN 1-56763-809-0 (hc)
              1-56763-810-4 (pbk)

    1. Horses—Juvenile fiction. [1. Horses—
Fiction. 2. Fourth of July—Fiction.
3. Patriotism—Fiction. 4. United States—
History—Fiction.] I. Sargent, Pat, 1936–
II. Lenoir, Jane, 1950– ill. III. Title. IV. Series.

    PZ7.S2465Fr 2004
    Fic]—dc21   2001008635

Printed in the United States of America

Inspired by

spotted grey horses we sometimes see in beautiful green fields.

Dedicated to

all children with freckles.
Be proud!
Freckles are special!

Foreword

When Big Boss Dave, owner of the Rocking S Horse Ranch, chooses Freckles the flea-bitten grey to carry the American flag in a Fourth of July celebration, Freckles is very proud. He is proud to carry Old Glory!

Contents

If you would like to have the authors of the Saddle Up Series visit your school, free of charge, call 1-800-321-5671 or 1-800-960-3876.

One

The July 4 Celebration

The Rocking S Horse Ranch bustled with activity. Cowboys arranged long tables in front of the barn as the women prepared good food and drinks to set on them. "Hmmm," thought Freckles the flea-bitten grey as he watched the happy folks work. "This is a special day for horses and folks on the Rocking S. I sure hope Big Boss Dave chooses me for the job of honor."

"Wow!" a loud voice behind him exclaimed. "I don't know what

1

all the fuss is about, but I sure do like celebrations."

Freckles turned around and smiled at the silver grullo.

"Me, too," he said, "especially since this celebration is honoring our grandfathers and grandmothers."

"Really?" the grullo gasped. "Why? What did they do?"

The flea-bitten grey glared at the grullo before snorting, "Humph! 'What didn't they do?' would be an easier question to answer. You see, this is July 4th–Independence Day. The United States of America would not be an independent nation without the help of us horses."

"Oh, that's easy to understand," the silver grullo said. "I didn't know that. I just thought this country was always free and fun."

"Humph," Freckles snorted again. "Your old forefathers worked long and hard to make things safe and good for you."

Suddenly their conversation was interrupted by loud cheers from all of the folks on the Rocking S.

Freckles turned around to look for the cause of the commotion. He saw the ranch foreman and one of the hired hands walking backward and staring up at two tall poles proudly displaying American flags. Between the waving symbols of freedom and pride, a large banner with bright red letters proclaimed:

WELCOME TO THE
ROCKING S HORSE RANCH
INDEPENDENCE DAY
RODEO AND PICNIC

"Wow," the silver grullo said.
"This must be a really special day.
The bosses are excited and happy."
Freckles smiled and nodded.

"They should be excited and happy," he said in a quiet voice. "The Rocking S horses played a very important role in the establishment of the United States of America."

"They did?" the grullo grunted. "Er...we did?"

"Of course," the flea-bitten grey said in a matter-of-fact tone. "Behind every pioneer in American history, there is a good horse."

The sound of singing voices suddenly drowned out his words.

Oh say can you see,
by the dawn's early light,
what so proudly we hailed
at the twilight's last gleaming...

"What did a horse have to do with that song?" the grullo asked with a chuckle. "We aren't noted for musical talent."

"A whole bunch," Freckles said. "Chet Chestnut's boss wrote 'The Star Spangled Banner.' Now, that's an inspirational story, Grullo."

"Tell me the story," the grullo said in an excited voice.

Before Freckles had a chance to speak, teams pulling wagons and buggies began arriving at the ranch. Children squealed with delight as they ran toward the long tables.

The saddled horses joined the harness rigs, and they nickered greetings while their bosses shook hands with friends and neighbors.

The flea-bitten grey pawed the ground with one front hoof as he watched the happy reunion.

He looked all around, eyeing every man there. "I really hope," he muttered to himself, "that I am the chosen one."

"What are you talking about?" the grullo asked with a very puzzled expression on his face.

"Never mind," Freckles said. "Let's go visit with our guests."

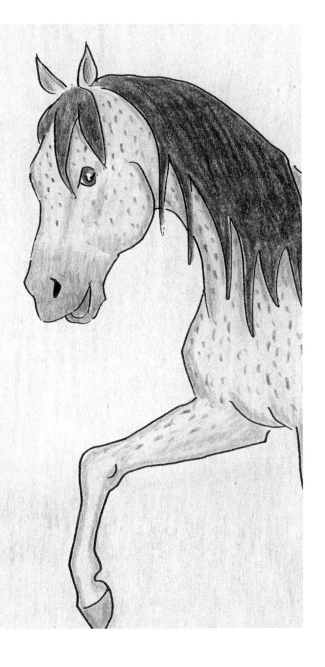

Two hours later, the celebration was in full swing. All the folks were laughing and talking and eating as the children chased barrel hoops or played hide-and-seek.

Every once in a while, a lucky horse received a bite of carrot or a lump of sugar from one of the kids.

"I love the Fourth of July," the grullo said as he crunched a sweet treat between his teeth.

"Me, too," Freckles murmured. "I think it's a great way to honor our forefathers." He switched his tail and added, "Plus a whole lot of fun!"

Two

Horses and U.S. History

The sun was high overhead when a young man with a fiddle and another with a guitar appeared on the scene. Moments later, the air was filled with happy music. Within a very short time, folks were singing and dancing all over the place. The silver grullo tapped a hoof while Freckles swayed gently with the music.

"Tell me more about famous horses and our American history, Freckles," the silver grullo said.

The flea-bitten grey nickered, "Well, you've probably heard about Dan the dappled mahogany bay and his boss, Paul Revere."

Freckles didn't notice the grullo shaking his head as he continued to speak. "And I'm sure you know the story of Duke the dappled palomino and the signing of the Declaration of Independence."

Again, Freckles failed to see the silver grullo shake his head. "And you've heard the story of Ring Silver and his boss, President Cleveland, when the Statue of Liberty was put in place."

Freckles stopped and rubbed his nose against his knee for a moment, and then his ears shot forward.

"Maybe you haven't heard about Popcorn Blue Corn and his boss, President Thomas Jefferson." Then the flea-bitten grey shook his head and added, "No. I'm sure you know about the Louisiana Purchase.

15

But," he said excitedly, "maybe you haven't heard the great story about Speck the black patterned leopard and his boss, Betsy Ross!"

As the silver grullo shook his head, Freckles said, "No. You know all about the origin of Old Glory."

Suddenly the silver grullo reared up on his hind legs and lashed at the air with his front hooves.

"Stop, Freckles!" he neighed. "You're driving me absolutely crazy. I don't know any of those stories. And," he snorted, "I never will if you don't tell me."

"Oh," Freckles groaned. "I can't do that, my friend. It would take me all day to tell you every one of those stories, and I want to enjoy the Rocking S celebration. But," he added cheerfully, "remind me to tell you about Sugar Cream and her boss, Benjamin Franklin." He chuckled as he added, "That little mare had a wonderful story to share."

The silver grullo glared and snorted, "Oh, yeah. Right. And I suppose I'll wonder about it from now on."

Freckles again ignored the testy attitude of his friend.

"And then there was Biscuit. That skewbald led an interesting life with his boss, George Washington. Biscuit watched as bosses signed the Constitution of the United States of America. He said they set the rules for how to be a proud and honorable American."

After pausing for a moment, he began to chuckle. "And Buckshot the blue-eyed chestnut," Freckles sputtered. "Buckshot was forever upset that Theodore Roosevelt did not take him to San Juan with the Rough Riders. But now, personally, I think Buckshot was lucky that he didn't have to ride the high seas in a big ship."

"Wow!" the silver grullo said. "That sounds like an exciting tale from American history."

"It is," Freckles agreed. "Every tale from our forefathers is exciting. From Cactus Jack the smoky black and Boss Annie Oakley to Nick the linebacked claybank dun and his boss, Wyatt Earp, horses have been a big part of the old frontier and how the west was won."

Suddenly Big Boss Dave, the ranch foreman, and another man walked up to the corral and looked at Freckles. "Hmmm," the flea-bitten grey thought. He smiled and nodded his head toward Big Boss Dave.

"I sure hope he picks me," he muttered as he raised his head and pointed his ears toward them.

"Who is that man with the ranch foreman?" the grullo asked quietly. "He looks important. Do you know him, Freckles?"

"Humph," Freckles snorted. "Your head has been in a feed bucket too long. Big Boss Dave owns the Rocking S. He's the grand marshal over the rodeo this afternoon."

Freckles tried to forget the testy silver grullo for a minute. He turned his attention to Big Boss Dave and the ranch foreman. He watched the men for several minutes. It was very obvious that they were trying to decide on a horse for a special job.

"If I want to be the chosen one," he thought, "I'd better strut my stuff and show them how classy I can look."

And a second later, Freckles was proudly prancing around the corral with his tail and mane flowing against the breeze. He was indeed a sight to behold.

"He's a good-looking horse," Big Boss Dave declared as the flea-bitten grey skidded to a halt in front of him.

"His name is Freckles," the ranch foreman said with a smile. "He is one of the smartest horses ever raised on the Rocking S, Boss. I think you'll find him easy riding and level headed."

"Listen to your ranch foreman, Big Boss Dave," Freckles whinnied softly as he nuzzled him on the cheek. "He's a good man. I've always known that, but I guess I just didn't realize until now that he is also a good friend of mine."

Three

Freckles Carries Old Glory

Two hours later, folks were slowly moving toward the arena. The flea-bitten grey felt his heart sink with disappointment as he watched the cowboys working near the roping and bucking chutes.

"I must not be the chosen one," he said quietly. "Big Boss Dave must have decided to ride Palomino instead of me."

A tear trickled down his face, and he quickly wiped it on his knee. "What's wrong with me?" he groaned. "This is our nation's day to be happy and proud. Shame, shame on me for standing here feeling sorry for myself!" His head went high in the air, and his ears shot forward.

"I am an American horse," he neighed loudly. "And I'm proud of it, even if I'm not the chosen one."

His thoughts were interrupted by a loud chuckle, and he jerked around to see who was laughing.

"How did you know, Freckles?" the foreman asked. "No horse can look as happy and proud as you." He paused before adding, "Unless you overheard Big Boss Dave and me talking a minute ago."

"Huh?" Freckles nickered. "I don't know what you're talking about, Ranch Boss. I just happen to feel happy and proud."

The ranch foreman patted him on the neck and said, "Come on, big fellow. We need to get you brushed and curried before the grand entry starts. Big Boss Dave has chosen you to carry the flag."

Once again a tear sneaked from the corner of his eye and slowly slid down his nose.

"Wow! Big Boss Dave really chose me?"

"But we must hurry and get you brushed and saddled," the foreman said as he quickly slipped the halter over Freckles's head.

"What's happening, Freckles?" the silver grullo nickered. "Where are you going? Aren't you going to watch the rodeo?"

The flea-bitten grey smiled and nodded his head.

"I'll watch it," he replied. "This is the most important rodeo in my life, and I wouldn't miss it for the world. Just try and remember the history I told you about. See you later, my friend."

"Good grief," the silver grullo murmured. "You told me a bunch in a short time. I'll never remember all of that horse history." He walked closer to the arena before adding, "But you can explain it to me again another time, Freckles."

It was forty-five minutes later when Big Boss Dave swung his right leg over the back of the saddle. After patting Freckles on the neck, he slid the flag into the boot that was hanging from the saddle horn. The flea-bitten grey gasped with emotion as he watched the banner unfurl.

Seconds later, Freckles entered the arena in a lope with the Stars and Stripes proudly waving above him.

The flea-bitten grey's hooves pounded against the firm sod as he circled the large enclosure twice.

"Hmmm," he thought. "Old Glory honors every horse and frontiersman from the Pony Express to the good country doctors to the explorers to each and every American hero from sea to shining sea." He skidded to a halt on his hind legs in front of the grandstand. As every man, woman, child, and horse pledged allegiance to the flag of the United States of America, Freckles neighed loudly, "Life is great! I am proud to be an American horse!"

Four

Flea-bitten Grey Facts

The color grey is a mixture of white hairs with colored body and point hairs. Grey horses are usually born colored. They become whiter every time they shed.

Greys are different in the color-naming scheme, because the color of the horse is not used in the name.

Many grey horses have a light mane and tail, while others have a dark mane and tail. Older greys may be mostly white or may have a dark mane and tail.

When small spots of color appear in the coat, the horse is called a flea-bitten grey.

Flea-bitten Grey

BEYOND "THE END"

There is something about the outside of a horse that is good for the inside of a man.
Sir Winston Churchill

LASSO THE ODD WORD
1. stallion   2. foal   3. filly
4. colt   5. mare   6. pastern

1. mane comb   2. withers
3. dandy brush   4. hoof pick
5. rubber currycomb   6. body brush

1. barrel   2. dock   3. fetlock
4. flaxen   5. hoof   6. flank

Copy the three groups of words. Five of the words in each group match or go together. Find the odd word and lasso it (Draw a circle around it.)!

CURRICULUM CONNECTIONS

Freckles knew all about many of the early leaders of his country. He told about the horses and their bosses who helped form the United States of America. These stories and horse characters are fiction, coming from the imagination of the authors, Dave and Pat Sargent. However, the events and "bosses" are real, based on true facts from the history of our country—historical fiction.

Who is the "boss" or leader of your school? What does he or she do?

Who are the leaders of your town or city, the state where you live, and the United States? What do they do?

Have any of the leaders you know done something that might inspire an author to write a book about them 200 years later?

Freckles was very proud to watch Old Glory unfurl and to lope around the arena with the stars and stripes waving above him. Like Freckles, take pride in the heroes of our country—learn about them and the flag that honors each and every one from sea to shining sea.

Be a proud American.

Learn to say the Pledge of Allegiance and to sing "The Star Spangled Banner."

Honor, respect, and be willing to defend our flag. The flag has a message for you at <www.massar.org/oldglory.htm>.

PROJECT

Combine your math and artistic skills!
Draw to scale and accurately color a picture (body, tail, and mane) of the horse
that is featured in each book read in the
Saddle Up Series. You could soon have
sixty horses prancing around the walls of
your classroom!

Learning + horses = FUN.

Look in your school library media center
for books about how to draw a horse and
the colors of horses. Don't forget the
useful information in the last chapter of
this book (Flea-bitten Grey Facts) and
the picture on the book cover for a shape
and color guide.

HELPFUL HINTS AND WEBSITES

A horse is measured in hands. One hand
equals four inches. Use a scale of 1"
equals 1 hand.

Visit website <www.equisearch.com> to find a glossary of equine terms, information about tack and equipment, breeds, art and graphics, and more about horses. Learn more at <www.horse-country. com> and at <www.ansi.okstate.edu/ breeds/horses/>.

KidsClick! is a web search for kids by librarians.   There are many interesting websites here.   HORSES and HORSE-MANSHIP are two of the more than 600 subjects.   Visit <www.kidsclick.org>.

Is your classroom beginning to look like the Rocking S Horse Ranch?   Happy Trails to You!

ANSWERS   (Lasso the odd word: Group 1, PASTERN is a point of a horse, others are ages; Group 2, WITHERS is a point of a horse, others are grooming tools; Group 3, FLAXEN is a color, others are points of a horse.)